MYSTERY
D · A · Y

BY HARRIET ZIEFERT
ILLUSTRATED BY
RICHARD BROWN

LITTLE, BROWN AND COMPANY   BOSTON   TORONTO

Sally

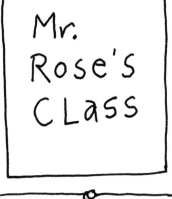

Mr. Rose's Class

Jennifer

Richard

Adam

Emily

Mr. Rose

Matt

Jamie

Kelly

Justin

Sarah

First Edition

Library of Congress Cataloging-in-Publication Data
Ziefert, Harriet
    Mystery day/by Harriet Ziefert; illustrated by Richard Brown.
        p. cm.—(Mr. Rose's class)
    Summary: Mr. Rose's class's experiment in identifying "mystery
powders" turns into a delicious chemistry lesson.
    ISBN 0-316-98769-7
    [1. Schools—Fiction.   2. Science—Experiments—Fiction.]
I. Brown, Richard Eric, 1946–   ill. II. Title.
III. Series: Ziefert, Harriet.   Mr. Rose's class.
PZ7.Z487Mz   1988
[E]—dc19

Published simultaneously in Canada
by Little, Brown & Company (Canada) Limited

Printed in Singapore for Harriet Ziefert, Inc.

For my first teachers—
    Samuel Margolin, Sylvia Margolin,
    Isaac Godlin, Helen Hudak

CHAPTER ONE
MYSTERY POWDERS

"Good morning, class! It's Friday,"
    said Mr. Rose.
"Good morning, Mr. Rose."
"I know this is Mystery Day," said Mr. Rose,
    "and you're ready to get to work.
        But first I have an announcement."
    Somebody groaned.

"No need to moan and groan," continued
Mr. Rose. "My announcement is very short.
After we do our mystery project, we're
going to have a mystery guest."

"A mystery guest—who?"

"Oh, he won't tell!" said Jamie.
"He never does!"

"You're right," said Mr. Rose. "It would be
easy to tell you. But I know you'll be able
to figure it out for yourselves."

"How?" someone asked.

"I'll give you a clue," answered Mr. Rose.
"The mystery guest will use all but one
of the mystery powders to make something
for all of you."

"But what if we can't figure it out?" Jamie asked.

"Don't worry, you will," promised Mr. Rose.
"First, let's talk about what you have to do."

"I know what we have to do," said Sarah,
pointing to the five pails on the table.
"We have to guess what the mystery powders
are—then prove it!"

"That's a good answer, Sarah," said Mr. Rose.

"But how would you do that?"

"I would look at them carefully," Sarah answered.

"What else could you do?" Mr. Rose asked.

Other kids raised their hands.

"You could smell them."

"You could feel them."

"You could mix them with water."

"Or, you could find the boxes they came in and match the powders with what's inside the boxes!"

"But that's cheating!" said Richard.

"Not necessarily," said Mr. Rose.

"Sometimes it's a good idea to match and compare something you *don't* know with something you *do* know.

But you still need to smell, and touch, and mix...."

"And taste!" said Sarah proudly.

Mr. Rose interrupted.

"Since I know the mystery powders are *not*
poisonous, Sarah's idea is a good one.
You can taste these powders in small amounts—
but *do not swallow* them. And never taste
anything unless you know it's safe."

"If these powders are safe, why can't we
swallow them?" Richard asked.
"Your taste buds will react to tiny, tiny
amounts," Mr. Rose answered. "These
powders are not food for your stomachs.
They are food for your brains.
Something for you to think about.
You'll get real food later."
"Is that another clue to the mystery guest?"
"Maybe yes, maybe no," Mr. Rose answered.

Mr. Rose called one group at a time
to the mystery table.
Jennifer and Kelly were first.
They put four spoonfuls of each powder
into paper sandwich bags.
"Is this enough?" Kelly asked, holding
a bag in the air.
"Yes, it's enough," said Mr. Rose.
"If you need more, you can always get some."

Richard, Matt, and Emily spooned their
powders and went back to their table.
Richard looked at the worksheet Mr. Rose
had left at his place.
"This looks easy," he said.
   "I'll be able to fill it out—
   one, two, three!"
"Don't be so sure," said Matt.
   "Mr. Rose never gives us anything
   that's too easy!"
Emily agreed.
"Just look at these powders," she said.
   "They're all the same color—white!"
"Not really!" said Richard. "There's
   grayish white, and yellowish white,
   and whiteish white!"
"Good observing," said Mr. Rose.
   "The 'white' powders are actually
   many shades of white."

Sarah, Sally, and Justin had been
waiting a long time.
They quickly filled their bags
and returned to their table.
"Let's taste Powder Number Two,"
    suggested Sarah.
"Let's do it together," said Sally.
    "Let's taste on the count of three.
    Remember, don't swallow!
    One, two, three...taste!"
"SALT!" they shouted together.
"That was easy," said Justin.
    "Let's try Powder Number Three next."
Justin wasn't sure he wanted to taste it.
"It looks and smells like plaster," he said.
"I think it's flour," said Sally.
"I think you're wrong," said Sarah.
    "I think it's baking soda."
Who was right?
Justin and Sally and Sarah would have
to experiment to find out.

Adam and Jamie were racing to their
table when Adam dropped a bag.
"Dummy!" someone shouted.
"Get the dust pan!"
"Here's the broom. Start sweeping!"
Mr. Rose's class was busy.
Busy with powders.
And the classroom floor would never
look quite the same again!

CHAPTER TWO
MIXING AND TESTING

Mr. Rose stood behind the mystery table.
He had put out small bottles
of vinegar and iodine.
There were eyedroppers,
magnifying lenses, and paper cups
half-filled with water.

"By now you should have put your guesses
on your worksheets," said Mr. Rose.
"Now I want you to prove that your
guesses are right with some simple tests."
Jennifer and Kelly decided to work together.
Mr. Rose said it was okay.
They got five cups of water from the table.
They put their worksheet in front of them.

POWDER #	GUESS	Reason
1	Flour	It's dusty It blows like it.
2	Salt	I tasted it. It's salty.
3	Sugar	It's sweet. It feels grainy
4	Plaster	It didn't taste good.
5	Baking Soda	It look like Flour. I've gargled with it!

"Let's test these powders in order,"
suggested Jennifer.

"Okay," said Kelly. "I put a spoonful
of flour into the cup."
"It makes the water cloudy," said Jennifer.
"And some of it floats on the top."
"May I pour in the salt now?" Kelly asked.
"No," answered Jennifer. "It's *my* turn!"
"Then I get to do the sugar," said Kelly.

Jennifer and Kelly poured.
"Look!" said Jennifer. "The salt just went
into the water and disappeared."
"The sugar disappeared, too!" said Kelly.
Mr. Rose heard the conversation.
He said, "When a solid disappears into
a liquid, we say it dissolves."
As he walked toward another table, Mr. Rose
added, "Do you think the salt and the
sugar *really* disappeared?"
A good question.
Something for Jennifer and Kelly
to think about.

Richard, Matt, and Emily were testing
with iodine.

Mr. Rose had them put newspaper on their
table because iodine can be messy.

Richard squeezed three drops onto
a spoonful of flour.

"Wow!" he said. "Look at this! First it turned
red. Now it's turning blue-black."

"I want to try it, too," said Matt.

"So do it!" said Richard. "I'm not stopping you."
Emily tried putting iodine on the salt.
Nothing happened.
Then she tried the baking soda.

"Look at this!" she yelled.

"I made mustard!"

"Oh, it's not really mustard," said Matt.
"It just looks like mustard. Give *me*
the eyedropper. I want to see if I can
make it turn yellow and orange, too."

Sarah, Sally, and Justin were testing
with vinegar.
They had all the powders in little cups
in front of them.
Mr. Rose gave them a question to answer—
*what powders can be identified most
easily with vinegar?*
They mixed each powder with vinegar—
starting with Powder Number Five.
Sarah asked the questions.
"What happens with salt?"
"Nothing much," answered Sally.
"What happens with plaster?"
"It's going to harden," answered Justin.
"What happens with sugar?"
"It dissolves," answered Justin and Sally.
"What happens with baking soda?"
"It fizzes!" they yelled together.
Sarah, Sally, and Justin knew
the answer to Mr. Rose's question.

Baking soda!
You can hear it fizz when the vinegar
and baking soda mix.
You have to listen carefully.
But you can hear it if you try.
Fizz.

Adam and Jamie were experimenting
with plaster and water.
"This is fun," said Adam.
"Yeah!" said Jamie.
She stuck her fingers into the goop.
"Maybe I can make a cast for my finger,"
    she said.
"You'd better add more water before it
    hardens," Adam warned.

Jamie poured more water.
She dumped in a whole cup.
"What are you doing?" Mr. Rose asked.
"I'm trying to keep this soupy so it
doesn't harden," Jamie answered.
"Here's a suggestion for you," said Mr. Rose.
"How long does it take for one teaspoon
of plaster mixed with one teaspoon of water
to harden? What if you use more water?
Less water? What if you use a flat dish?
A deep dish?"
"Enough!" said Jamie. "Enough questions!
Sometimes you give me too much to think about!"
"I'm sorry," said Mr. Rose. "Just think about
one question at a time. Then I'm sure
you'll have no trouble."

Mr. Rose gave Jennifer and Kelly pieces
of black construction paper.
They wanted to know which powder
was the powderiest.
Mr. Rose said they could find out by
rubbing some of each powder onto the
paper, then seeing how much remained when
they blew the loose powder away.

Jennifer said, "I like the feel of
    this one—it's smooth and silky."
"Not this one," said Kelly. "It's hard
    and grainy."
"It must be sugar!" said Jennifer.
"You're right," said Kelly. "Did you ever
    try to sleep with sugar in your bed?"
"Yuck!" said Jennifer.

Mr. Rose asked for everyone's attention.
"Stop working for a minute!" he said.
"But we're having fun!" said Justin.
"I'll only take sixty seconds of your time,"
    said Mr. Rose.

"He must have more questions," said Jamie.
Adam agreed.
Mr. Rose must have something else for his class
to think about.
Something harder.

Mr. Rose told the class he had prepared
some bags with not just one powder—
but with two or three different ones.
"This is your chance to experiment,"
    he said.
"But how?" someone asked.
"I know," said Justin. "We could use
    vinegar or iodine."
"Or we could use our tongues and our
    noses," said Adam.
"All of those ideas are good," said Mr. Rose.
    "I'll put a chart on the board to help
    everyone out."
Mr. Rose walked to the blackboard.
He printed a big chart.

Mr. Rose said, "Later everyone will have
a chance to make a mixture of two powders.
Then each of you can trade with a friend
and try to guess what the powders are."
Justin smiled.
He saw this as a chance to trick Kelly.
She would never guess the two powders
in the bag he would fix for her.

CHAPTER THREE
MYSTERY GUEST

"It's just about time for the mystery
    guest to arrive," said Mr. Rose.
    "Does anyone want to guess who's coming?"
"Is it a mad scientist?" Matt asked.
  Everyone laughed.
"I know," said Jamie. "It's a cook.
    And the cook is going to make a concoction!"
"What's that?" someone asked. "It sounds awful!"

"What does the dictionary say about
'concoction'?" asked Mr. Rose.
"I found it," cried Emily.
"It says under concoct: *to prepare
from crude materials; to prepare by
combining different ingredients.*"

"See? Crude materials—that means
nasty things," said Richard.

"Do you think the powders you worked with
today are nasty?" Mr. Rose asked.

Just then there was a knock on the door.

"It's the mystery guest!" Kelly yelled.

"Come in," called Mr. Rose.

A man walked into the classroom.

"Class, this is Mr. Peters," announced
Mr. Rose.

"Hello, Mr. Peters," the class said.

"Are you a cook?" Jamie asked.

"I'm a kind of cook," Mr. Peters answered.
"I'm a baker."

"Are you going to concoct something?"
Jamie went on.

"Yes, and each of you is going to help me."

"What's it going to be?" Matt asked.

"That's for me to know and for you to find
out," Mr. Peters said.

"You sound just like Mr. Rose!" said Kelly.

"I guessed who the mystery guest would be,"
Jamie bragged.

"So what?" said Richard. "He'll probably
make us something gross."

Mr. Peters unpacked a bag.

He put out an eggbeater, two bowls,

a big wooden spoon,

some measuring cups and spoons,

butter, eggs, vanilla, and brown sugar.

"Mr. Rose said you were going to use
the powders we tested today," said Jennifer.

"I am," said Mr. Peters. "But I have to add
a few more things to make them work together.
Now, I'm going to give each of you a task.
Who wants to go first?"

"I DO!" everyone shouted at once.

"I have an idea," said Mr. Rose. "Line up
next to the blackboard in alphabetical
order by first names. Walk. Don't run!"

Mr. Peters called Adam to the table.
He told Adam to measure a cup of butter
and put it into the mixing bowl.
"How do I do that?" Adam asked.
"Check the wrapper," said Mr. Peters.
    "What does it say?"
"It says that this stick is one-half cup
    of butter," Adam answered.
"So how many sticks are in a cup?"
  Adam thought for a minute.
"Two!" he said.
  Then he added the butter to the bowl.

Emily was next.

"Your job is to add Powder Number Three—
white sugar," said Mr. Peters. "We need
one cup."

Mr. Peters showed Emily how to measure
the sugar evenly.

She added it to the bowl with the butter.

Jamie put in one cup of brown sugar.
Then Mr. Peters helped her mix the
butter and sugar with his beater.

Jennifer and Justin each broke in an egg.
They mixed the eggs into the batter
until they almost disappeared.

Kelly added a teaspoon of vanilla.

"It smells delicious," Kelly said.

Mr. Peters agreed.

"It does smell good. But don't taste it.
Vanilla tastes terrible by itself."

Richard whispered to Sally, "I told you
he was going to make something nasty."

When it was Matt's turn, Mr. Peters said,
"Here's Powder Number One—flour.
It gives the dough body."

Matt put two cups into a second bowl.
This bowl was for the dry ingredients.

Richard added a teaspoon of Powder Number
Two—salt—to the flour.
He looked at the bowl with the wet ingredients.
"Whoever heard of putting salt and sugar together?"
    Richard asked.
"Salt cuts the sweetness of the sugar,"
    Mr. Peters explained.

Mr. Peters told Sally to put in a teaspoon
of Powder Number Five—baking soda.
'This is to make the dough rise a little,"
    he explained. "Now I'll mix the dry
    ingredients with the butter-sugar mixture."

Sarah frowned.
There were no ingredients left on the table.
"What do I get to do?" she asked. "We're
    not going to add plaster, are we?"
Mr. Peters laughed.

"No, no! But you do get to add something—
    the best ingredient of all!"
He pulled a small bag out of somewhere
    and handed it to Sarah.
"Chocolate chips! We're making chocolate chip
    cookies! They're my favorite," said Sarah.
"See, Richard?" said Jamie. "A concoction
    can be something yummy!"
Richard didn't mind being wrong this time.

After Sarah added the chocolate chips,
Mr. Peters mixed the batter one more time.

Then he let everyone help him put spoonfuls
of dough onto two cookie sheets.
"Don't put the dough too close together,"
he warned. "Leave room between the cookies.
The heat in the oven makes the dough
spread out."
"It would be fun to make one big cookie,"
said Matt.
"But how would we share it?" asked Sarah.
Matt teased, "We could break it with
a hammer or we could..."

Mr. Rose asked for everyone's attention.
"While the cookies bake in the lunchroom,
let's clean up the classroom," suggested
Mr. Rose.
"Do we have to?" Adam asked.
"You do if you want fresh-baked cookies,"
said Mr. Rose.
"You heard him—let's hurry up," Adam said
to his friends.

Justin reminded Mr. Rose, "You said we could mix two powders and make mystery bags."

"You're right, Justin. I guess we have time to do that now."

Justin smiled.

He didn't want to lose his chance to fool Kelly.

CHAPTER FOUR
MYSTERY MIXTURES

"Mr. Rose said, "I'm sure you don't want anyone
to see the mixture you are concocting.
So one person at a time at the mystery table."
"Thanks for the privacy!" said Kelly.

"You're welcome!" said Mr. Rose.
"As soon as everyone makes a mixture,
you can make your trades."
One by one people went to the table.
Some mixed quickly.
Some mixed slowly.
Then someone would shout, "Hurry up!
You're taking too long!"

Justin took longer than anyone.
What was he doing?
Was it something nasty?
Kelly would soon find out.

When everyone was finished, Mr. Rose
    announced, "Now it's trading time."
Richard traded with Matt.
Emily traded with Adam.
Sally traded with Sarah.
Jamie traded with Jennifer.
And Justin traded with Kelly.

Everyone got right to work.
Richard and Matt and Emily went
to the mystery table.
They examined their mystery mixtures.
"I'm going to make a mixture that looks just like
the one Matt gave me," said Richard.
"And I'm going to make a mixture exactly like
this one," said Matt, holding up his mystery bag.
"Me too!" said Emily.
So they went down the row of buckets,
dumping in a little of this and a little of that.
Matt said, "I think what Richard gave me was
flour, sugar, and baking soda, because what I made
looks just like what Richard concocted."
"Is Matt right?" Mr. Rose asked.
"He's almost right," said Richard.
"Except for the sugar."
"I guess I'll have to taste Richard's mixture,"
said Matt. "Then I'll get it right."
"Good idea," said Mr. Rose, "But remember,
a tiny bit on your tongue is enough."

57

Sarah and Sally decided to test
with vinegar and iodine.
Sarah was sure her mixture did not have
any flour in it—it did not turn black.
And Sally decided her mixture did have
a little baking soda in it.
"I hear a little fizz for a little baking soda,"
    said Sally with a grin.

Kelly was working hard to figure out
what was in the bag Justin gave her.
It did not have the taste of sugar.
It did not have the taste of salt.
It did not have the taste of baking soda.
It did not turn black—so there was no flour.
"You're not so smart," she said to Justin.
    "This bag is pure plaster!"

"Wrong!" said Justin with a smirk,
    "It's a mixture! And a mixture has
    two or more ingredients!"
"Well, you must have cheated," said Kelly.
    "Because this mixture doesn't have two
    of Mr. Rose's ingredients!"
"It does so!" insisted Justin. "It has
    Mr. Rose's plaster and . . .
    Mr. Rose's chalk dust!"
"You cheated!" yelled Kelly.
"I did not!" Justin yelled back.
"What's going on here?" asked Mr. Rose.
    "Whatever it is, I think this argument
    will have to be settled later."

Mr. Rose called for everyone's attention.
"Put everything away," he said.
It was time to get ready for the snack.
Kelly gave out the cups.
Matt passed around the napkins.
As a special treat, Mr. Rose had
two different kinds of juice.
Justin poured apple juice
for those who wanted it.
Emily poured fruit punch.
And nothing spilled.
Not one single drop!
"Where are the cookies?"
     asked Sarah. "I'm so hungry.
     I wish we could eat already!"
"Remember, Sarah," said Mr. Rose,
     "cookies take about fifteen minutes to bake."
"Will they be soft and chewy?" someone asked.
"I'm sure they'll be hard as rocks," teased Matt.
"Well, if they are," answered Sarah,
     "then I'll break a tooth!"
"Don't worry," said Mr. Rose,
     "I'm sure the cookies will be just right."

"What are we going to do next week?"
Matt asked.

"I have some good ideas," said Mr. Rose.
"But I'd rather keep them to myself."

"Please tell," Jennifer begged.

"You can wait," answered Mr. Rose.
"You can wait until Monday.
Right now, enjoy the cookies.
Then this class will be dismissed
for the weekend."

"Three cheers for Friday!" someone shouted.
"Three cheers for Mr. Peters!" said someone else.
"And three cheers for Mr. Rose!"

Homework

1 Test some other things with iodine — bread, lettuce potato chips, rice and powdered milk.

2 Test some other things with vinegar — milk, apple slices, and cream.

3 Ask an adult to share a favorite cookie recipe. Copy it. Bake the cookies, if you can.

Mr. Rose